HOW MUSIC SA`

by Antimo I

CW00517202

Introduction

In one of his aphorisms, the German philosopher Friedrich Nietzsche reminds us that *life would be a mistake without music*. In fact, it appears that music is what makes us human, and more so than other forms of art, it profoundly affects how we live our lives. Music stimulates parts of the brain that are involved in language and motor coordination, but also has a profound effect on our deepest thoughts and emotions, including both the pleasant ones, like joy, and the unpleasant, like fear.

From my early years to the present, music has played a major role in my life and continues to do so. It crowned my most beautiful dreams, makes me fall in love, provokes me to cry; it took me around the world and fished me out of the abyss of a nightmare. I also drew on it as a lifeline over a long period of isolation. I'll describe how music saved my life and influenced the decisions I made along my way.

This book has been written between London (on bus 185, 176, Jubilee and District underground line, Highbury &

Islington overground line, Victoria and Denmark Hill stations) and Manchester (UK), Caserta and Naples (Italy), Santa Cruz de Tenerife, Puerto de la Cruz, La Orotava, Sagunto, Valencia and Las Palmas (Spain), Béziers and Vias (France), Marrakech and Essaouira (Morocco) and somewhere else flying at a cruising altitude between ten and twelve thousand metres.

Antimo Magnotta

HOW MUSIC SAVED MY LIFE

My left eye

I'll be walking along invisible borderlands.
What is not seen, IS ...

Sorrento, Italy
Autumn 1971

Doctor D'Esposito, an eminent ophthalmologist and professor at the University of Naples, after a careful investigation, sank behind the large desk, put on his spectacles and checked his notes.

He had a slender body, thin legs and arms, a slightly elongated head and little hair.

His white medical coat looked a few sizes too big.

He gripped the typewriter for an instant like it was a helm, mentally compiled all the information gathered during the eye examination, fixed the sheet in the roller and immediately began to bang loudly on the keys.

From time to time some reflection led him to rest his gaze on certain objects scattered on the desk: paperweights, books, correspondence, magazines, framed photos.

Silence slipped in between reflections, interrupted only by the rustling of the large curtains dancing in the wind blowing from the Gulf of Naples.

The keystrokes on the typewriter sounded like a small automatic gun with which he cleared the field of any doubt.
His figure appeared very far behind the large and wide desk, his movements were slow and studied. From a distance it could appear as a slightly asymmetrical paper cutout.

His studio looked like a small cabinet of curiosities and extraordinary objects. There were drawings of large eyes, photos of pathologies, diplomas and certificates with Latin inscriptions, posters of anatomical parts on the walls, models of small skeletons posing grotesquely on the furniture, strange measuring instruments, lenses of various sizes, a microscope.

Many years later I would remember his slender figure when I came across Alberto Giacometti's sculptures for the first time.

The pounding on the typewriter keys stopped with a bicycle bell sound.
The piece of paper that contained the truth about my eyes was finally released from the captivity of the roller.
The doctor pulled the sheet out with a quick gesture, as if he were a slightly sullen orchestra conductor.

He placed the sheet on the desk, took off his spectacles and cleared his throat: "*Esotropia.* This child does not see very well, also his left eye is lazy, it is weaker than the right and tends to converge inwards. However, we can correct this squint with the right lenses, but only when he grows a little."

This was the sentence pronounced by the old ophthalmologist.

My mom was sitting on a chair opposite the doctor, listening carefully and hugging me. Her weary gaze didn't seem to belong to her young figure. After months, she still looked exhausted from the heroic labour of my birth.

My father, standing next to the chair, remained motionless as in a vintage photo.

The Gulf wind sneaked in through the large windows like an invisible dragon and seemed to animate all those still and funny objects in the studio.

Well, I was told that due to an extremely high body temperature at birth, I landed on this planet with poor vision.

But there's more.

The most bizarre occurrence during labour was a hilarious mishap.

Ouverture: *Allegro agitato*

Go Young Warrior, push and don't stop until you hear the screams!

I heard this story from my parents years later.
I was born at home, on a table, in a little Southern Italian community.
It was early in the afternoon of a scorching July. My mother was only twenty. She was there, along with my grandma and the village midwife, in the bedroom that had been turned into a delivery room for the occasion.
My grandfather and my uncle were the only men present at that time and they were both outside in the hallway. Dad was running back from work.
The midwife had prepared everything necessary, my mother had already gone into labour. She took deep breaths, started pushing and I began the march towards the world.
The universe was preparing to welcome me and it seemed that everything was ready for my arrival.
My mother was squirming on her back and giving birth to me when the table leg broke and the homemade theatrical apparatus of my birth began to trot.

Panic!

As soon as my uncle heard my mother screaming, he rushed into the bedroom and quickly jumped beneath the table to stop it from shattering as I was beginning to (scantily) see the light.

My mum was shrieking and writhing whilst pushing me out, the midwife trying to grab me, my grandmother in tears, my uncle under the table and my grandfather stood in the corridor in a frozen expression that resembled Munch's *Scream.*

What a spectacle of extravaganza!

Wasn't this the aesthetic quintessence, the pinnacle of the Italian *neorealism*? There was melodrama, fantasy, comedy. A scene that might have been in a Vittorio De Sica film!
My father arrived soon after: the first thing he did was to snap a polaroid photo. The image of my weary and transfigured young mother lying on the bed, gazing at me wrapped in swaddling clothes.
On the back of that polaroid he wrote: *the Warrior at rest, 27th of July 1971, 2.15 pm.*

I believe that the moment I was born, my life was already marked out.

It seemed as though the squeak of the movement, the yell, the crack of the table leg breaking, the people around the scene and my final birth cry were all leading up to something ... *unprecedented.*
There was a fairly unique soundtrack to my delivery.

The opening overture was certainly an *Allegro agitato.*

I don't know why, but I still think that I may have secretly known that I wanted to be a musician.

They called me **Antimo**, which derives from the Greek *Anthos* and means *similar to a blossoming flower*, then passed to the Latin *Anthimus* which means *he who does not like to be low.*

La Famiglia

Lots of people resided in the house: my parents, four children and two maternal grandparents, who actually weren't our real grandparents. In reality my mother's parents both died when she was rather young and she was adopted by her aunt, her real mother's sister, who married a baker from Naples, but never had children.

My mom kept calling them uncles, but to us they were Nonna and Nonno.

When I was at home I remember always feeling or sensing something moving. My mom and grandma were always busy, there was often a neighbour knocking on the door, the television's buzzing noise, the traffic and street vendors, the voices from the balconies around our building. A never-ending *concrete music* symphony.

So I had limited vision, but I **heard** everything very well and my head was always full of sounds.

Opposite where we lived there was a family of farmers where my mother sent me every now and then to buy milk directly from the source. The source was called Lulu, a huge cow spotted with white, brown and black patches with beautiful shading. I remember Lulu, who made very good milk and I still remember the pleasant sensation of warmth I felt when I touched the metal jug into which her milk was poured.

My father, every now and then, to lighten my mother's work, took us around on his bus on mountain roads, or to the sea.

The most unique character in the house was certainly my grandfather. He had been a baker as a young man then left for World War II, was taken prisoner of war, returned home a bit stoned and with a bullet in his calf. So he was sent into early retirement, but he never stopped making bread.

They said he never went to school, but that he was a genius of the oven - a true master baker.

It is from him that my mother learned the job.

He was quite a reserved and taciturn type, taking care of his own small garden, he had a passion for birds and I remember that every now and then in the evening he would gather all of us brothers in a corner of the house and tell us stories about when he was at war.

My grandfather spoke only in the Neapolitan dialect, he didn't know the Italian language well.

Some of his tales seemed authentic, others completely made up.

He often began the stories with "When I was in Africa during the war..." Even though I knew the stories by heart, I liked listening to him and he always made me smile. He told of when, during the Second World War, he was a soldier of

17

some Italian regiment lost who knows where in Africa where he was a motorcyclist delivering the mail between various military garrisons. Unfortunately, he often ended up with the bike broken down, lost on some desert dune around there. Luckily there was always someone who went to rescue him. Or he told of when he helped the African women of the village near the regiment to give birth, when he taught the *Negus* to play Neapolitan cards, or when he entertained his fellow soldiers by building ships in bottles with bits of wood and scraps of cloth.

"Hey Grandpa, who was the *Negus*? And how did you understand each other when speaking different languages?"

"I don't remember exactly…but it was an important one. He understood me, he wasn't stupid".

"Grandpa, how did you help the women of the African village to give birth?"

"You're too young to understand… I'll explain it to you when you're older".

But for him that age never came.

I wondered many years later just how he had acquired all those skills, from motorcycling to village midwifery, to constructing ships in bottles. At home with us he was a relatively lazy and taciturn type who didn't stand out for his particular faculties. They just said he was a good baker.

However, my grandfather's stories were always wrapped in mystery and he never indulged in explanatory details. The story was the story, period. There was no need to explain.

It was precisely this peculiarity that had always fascinated me. When I listened to him I felt like the archetypal circus tightrope walker balancing on that thin line between truth and fantasy.

His stories, even if they were always the same, have remained with me for years, those indelible images imprinted in my memory.

Oh yes, I remember my Nonno, who died too early. Thin, silent, with that eternal cigarette half dangling from his lip. At home you would find him near you without feeling his presence, hearing his footsteps or his voice from afar. He seemed to materialise in a corner suddenly, like a spirit.

I have a rare photo of him posing in the bakery with his workers, my grandmother and my mother as a baby.

I loved my Nonno, the most questionable of storytellers.

My first *Klingmann*

I can still hear the gravel crunching under my feet
as I walked through the garden.
I loved that sound and I thought this must be music, too!

I was a quiet child who didn't speak much, but was incredibly curious about everything.

When I was six years old, I asked my parents to learn to play the piano. I had seen someone do it on television and it fascinated me.

There have never been musicians in my family. I am the son of a bus driver and a baker and I am the eldest of four children.

Only my paternal grandfather, a bricklayer, occasionally played the mandolin and sang popular Neapolitan songs during breaks for the workers on the construction site where he worked. His intention was pure, with an almost Hellenic, cathartic purpose: to play for enchantment and relieve the fatigue of his fellow workers.

I lived with my family in Recale, not very far from Naples, a community of a few thousand inhabitants scattered around the four main roads which all converged on the *piazza* in the centre of the town. We all knew each other.

They took me to Signora Giovanna, the only piano teacher in town. This lady was the owner of an immense villa with a beautiful garden, a kind of impregnable fortress where she lived with her family of noble origins. She led an almost monastic life and rumour has it that she was widowed at a very young age and had two daughters that no one knew about.

That afternoon my father knocked on the heavy and wide wooden door which slowly opened onto a vast courtyard. There were several rooms overlooking it and the sound of a piano came from one of them. I was utterly bewitched.
The maid took us to the studio where Signora Giovanna was waiting for me at the piano.
The pupils of her piano school with their parents were escorted to the room for the lesson and back to the front door at the end of it. They were the only ones who could access her villa.
My parents waited in a small sitting room and I was left alone with her and the piano.
"This child has a marked inclination for music. I made him sit down at the piano and he didn't want to leave. As far as I'm concerned, we can begin the lessons" she reported to my parents who stood jaw-dropped in awe.

I have hazy recollections of my initial encounter with Signora Giovanna. But I do recall that her home gave me the impression of a haunted museum.

Large keys hanging on the wall, old furniture, candles on the piano and all those artworks. Everything seemed to be so ancient.
Every now and then, I caught a glimpse of a shadow moving through one of the door's thick frosted glass. Maybe it was her maid…

Everyone in the village knew Pietro, Signora Giovanna's gardener, a grumpy deaf-mute … but, they said, a true connoisseur of plants and flowers. Occasionally he could be seen outside at the bar in the central piazza drinking a beer, immersed in his own deep silence.

The mystery surrounding the Lady undoubtedly contributed to local rumours and gossip. Paradoxically, a deaf-mute was the sole reliable eyewitness to the villa of secrets. The poor gardener, who saw everything that was happening inside that mysterious fortress, couldn't tell anything about it.
Given this circumstance, the investigation about the Lady became considerably more challenging as a result.
When some male at the bar made gestural allusions to the Lady's daughters, he received only odd grunts and grimaces from Pietro in return.

On a late autumn afternoon in 1977 several people in Recale noticed the arrival of the truck carrying my first piano. Our apartment was on the ground floor, in a three-storey building where two other families lived, those of my father's brother and sister.
We were eleven cousins in that building, all male. A female cousin arrived by surprise after a long interval.
The piano was placed in the living room of our house which had a large window overlooking the street. That afternoon all

my cousins gathered at that window to see what that mysterious delivery was.

...What's that kind of shiny black cabinet?
It was a brand new upright *Klingmann*. My first piano.

My mother claims that it was quite challenging to keep my cousins away from that window when I practised the piano in the afternoons. They frequently knocked on it and asked if I would play football with them on the street.
"When will you be done?!?"

To keep them away, my grandmother who lived with us would stand guard brandishing a broom during my daily piano practice.
She resembled a knight assigned to protect the shrine.

My journey with the piano had begun.

Magic powers

Having trouble seeing required me to wear bulky spectacles, which made me feel uncomfortable and shy. However, I was a happy kid.

The unexpected visions that music provided let me see things very differently.

That new world was magnificent to me and far more stunning than the real one.

Bach, Clementi, and Mozart were the first classical piano works I learned to play.

My family gathered around the piano when I performed as though I were the master of an intriguing ceremony.

Music seemed to endow me with magical abilities.

Despite my poor eyesight, I read a lot and asked many questions.

I believe my nonstop queries caused my parents a bit of stress so they eventually bought me an encyclopaedia called *A Thousand Questions,* a concentrated body of knowledge in just three volumes, bound in crimson leather with gold letters embossed on the spine. I can still recall the smell of it.

I hunched over those books and committed to learn by heart the names of the most remote rivers, the capital cities of far-off nations and intriguing details about exotic cultures. My mum took care of returning me home from my imaginary trips around the world with a dry and thunderous *"**Supper's ready**!"* after I had ideally gone throughout the globe from my tiny desk like a little explorer.

Me, the piano and the encyclopaedia *A Thousand Questions* were the only things on my make-believe deserted island.
"One day I'll leave and go see all these places in person" I used to tell myself all the time.
But music ruled the day and quickly took centre stage in my life. I could have given up going on afternoon raids with my various brothers and cousins or playing football in the street, but never my hours spent playing the piano in the company of Bach, Clementi and Mozart.

My mom was quite popular in the village because of her job as a baker. At school I was now *Antimo-the-son-of-the-baker-who-plays-the-piano* and this also earned me some respect. When we played ball or other sports in general during gym class at school, my classmates were careful not to push me or hit me on the hands. "Guys - watch out for his hands, this guy plays the piano!" That kindness put a smile on my face.

My first concert

Plants listen and remember.
Who knows how many sounds they hear, how many stories they have
eavesdropped on, perfectly camouflaged like secret agents, how much life
they take in.
Stories of winds, sunrises, birds, insects, sunsets, daydreams, clouds, sea.
The music of the days going by, the infinite symphony of time.
I wish they could speak one day whilst we stay still and listen. I'm sure
they could tell us more than we would ever know about ourselves. Of our
roots sunk into time like theirs in the soil.
I will play for them today.
I want them to remember me.

My very first public appearance as a pianist took place in Signora Giovanna's beautiful garden. All of her students performed in a summer concert. Twenty of us, ranging in skill from beginners to the more advanced.

I recall Pietro the factotum setting up the piano in the middle of the lawn and when the concert started, he remained still in a nearby corner for the entire extended afternoon of music. His figure resembled one of the several trees in the garden. He occasionally grinned and nodded his head and probably didn't hear the music, but in my opinion he heard it in the same way that a tree would. Perhaps the music was able to reach him through the furrows of his skin, which was wrinkled like the trunk of an oak, and lifted his spirits a little.

It was 1979, I was eight years old and I played a minuet by Bach and a sonatina by Clementi.

Signora Giovanna was a perfect event planner. She took care of the smallest detail.
At dusk, all of the students' parents were seated in that magnificent garden, smiling and looking happy. Some peered about in the hopes of catching a glimpse of the Villa of Secrets or to sneak a peek at the Lady's daughters dancing amid the woods like nymphs of the forest.

However, not even a shadow of them was ever noticed.
Cocktails were also served before and after the performance. It was like being in a late 19th century painting.

That summer the concert in the villa quickly became a catchphrase in the main bar of the piazza.

"But where have the two girls gone?" was a common question.

The earthquake

On November 23rd, 1980, there was a terrible earthquake: the epicentre was in Irpinia, not very far from my town.

That evening I was out playing with a friend of mine when I felt the iron and glass balconies of our building shake. All of a sudden I saw lots of people fleeing down the street. My parents and grandparents ran out of our house with my siblings in their arms. One of them, my brother Gianluca, was missing. He had camped out beneath some furniture to play.
My father went back and promptly rescued him.
"What about my piano?" I asked my mum.
"Don't worry, dad covered it with a big cloth", which was what I needed to hear.
Luckily none of us were hurt, our house was not damaged and my piano survived the earthquake.

For a week, we slept in two cars, and during the evenings, we would spend time with all of my cousins and relatives around the fire that one of my uncles had lit outside his garage, which was a distance from the building where we were housed.

What a terrifying event! The earth trembled, I could hear a maddening orchestra of timpani, double basses and brass playing incessant crescendos.

We returned to normal life after a few weeks and I naturally resumed studying.

I began to play in public more frequently, to participate in piano competitions and even to write some pieces.

The piano was now my travel and life companion.

Growing up

Years went by, I was now a teenager: my piano repertoire began to be a little more challenging.

I began to approach pieces like Schubert's *Impromptus*, Debussy's *Children's Corner* and some Bach preludes and fugues.

Signora Giovanna was very proud of me.

But the time had come to change something, according to her.

"You will soon have to leave here," the Lady told me one day.

My piano adventure began with her when I was six years old, and the heavy wooden front door of her villa closed behind me for the last time one afternoon in June. I was almost thirteen.

That afternoon, after the piano lesson in the villa, Pietro waited for me right in the middle of the courtyard, standing still like a horseless carriage. He accompanied me to the door, raised a hand and nodded his head.

"Ciao Pietro, take care of yourself".

After giving me one final hug, Signora Giovanna introduced me to one of her former students, Francesca. She was going to be my new piano teacher.

When I first walked in Francesca's studio, the air was filled with the aroma of freesias.

Her voice reminded me of the wind, and she had incredibly long, black hair.

I think she was in her thirties.

We started with *Ballade* No. 1 in G minor by Chopin. She said that piece was perfect for me. We then added the *Kinderszenen* collection by Schumann, a sonata by Haydn, one by Mozart and other compositions by Bach.

Her elderly mother occasionally brought me orange juice during the piano lessons.

Due to chronic tendonitis, Francesca was no longer able to play the piano, so she made the decision to focus solely on teaching. She had an evident preference for romantic and impressionistic music.

When I entered her piano room for the lesson, there was usually this ethereal, melancholic music playing on the stereo, which over time, along with the aroma of freesias, started to make me queasy.

I could easily visualise Marcel Proust sitting by the window writing his *Recherche du Temps Perdu,* whilst the room's golden dust drifted over Debussy's compositions in the slanted afternoon light.

Meanwhile my adolescence was knocking on my heart and body with vigour. More music began to enter my ears as well and new curiosities began to dawn. Many of my piano classmates turned up their noses at the thought of listening to any music other than classical. In contrast, for me, music has always been an organic *whole.* No distinction or snobbery, just music.

The **80s**! The world was changing, new fashion, music that perfectly mirrored that lightheartedness, a strong economy and a great deal of hope.

We were happy, or at least optimistic.

Here came Duran Duran, U2, Gino Vannelli, Spandau Ballet, Billy Idol, Whitney Houston, Wham! and many others that I was literally crazy about. I also listened to a lot of Italian music, my favourites being Pino Daniele, Lucio Battisti, Franco Battiato, Sergio Caputo, Donatella Rettore, Paolo Conte.

Duran Duran's *Wild Boys* was the first English song I learned by heart. Although I didn't fully get everything, using a little English to impress the females in my class was a fantastic tactic. I started to overcome my shyness by asking girls to dance at house parties to Billy Idol's *Eyes without a face*.

There was a run-down piano in my school's auditorium. Sometimes during the gymnastics hour I would sit and play something. Around that time, I learned George Michael's *Careless Whispers* and played it one day while most of my classmates were chasing a ball. After a while I became surrounded by a group of girls who held each other tightly and swayed softly to the music. I had absolutely no idea what the text was about - but the success was immediate. Wow!

Music gave me an edge; I was no longer that shy kid I used to be.

Meantime we moved into a new house, a much bigger one.
It was a villa that my father, his brother and my grandfather - the amateur mandolinist — had been building together. Everyone in the family participated in the construction work, even us little ones. We had to do simple tasks, for example carrying a few bricks, holding the water hose, fetching a few buckets of sand or the like.
In my eyes it was a huge mansion. Two floors and a small garden with a giant lemon tree in the backyard.
A new piano also arrived when the house was finished. My first *grand* piano, a secondhand Yamaha with a brilliant sound. It was placed on the first floor, in our new living room.

My cousins could no longer gather at the window. They lived a few streets away down in the village and we only saw each other on weekends, so my grandmother stopped guarding the temple with a broom to keep them away from my piano practice.

It was 1984.

A curious thing happened in pop culture that year, which quickly became an international scoop. While filming a shot for a Pepsi commercial, singer Michael Jackson was hit by sparks produced by a pyrotechnic effect and his hair caught fire.

For the first time, Doctor Robert Gallo isolated the AIDS virus in a laboratory.

Astronauts aboard the Space Shuttle Challenger in February of that year performed the first wireless spacewalk away from the orbiting station. As the New York Times reported: *Free of any lifeline and propelled into the dark void by tiny jets, they became the first human satellites.*

Eddy Murphy became the most famous actor on the planet.

On July 5, 1984, Diego Armando Maradona arrived in Naples. From that day on, the history of football and of that city changed. Diego took the Napoli football team to unprecedented heights and became something of a cult figure.

That summer, my mom bought two hundred kilos of tomatoes to make the classic sauce, as per tradition in southern Italy. The whole family participated in the production with the external contribution of a neighbour named Carmela, whose ambiguous past was the subject of heated debates and unbridled fantasies in the main bar of the piazza.
In the process of making the sauce, we four brothers were in charge of washing the bottles and picking the basil in the small backyard garden.

It turned out to be an exceptional year for that tomato sauce, the news of which even reached the bar of the piazza, overshadowing for a while the Napoli football matches, the investigations about Signora Giovanna's daughters, the gossip about Carmela and all the chatter evaporating in the heat of that scorching summer.

My new glasses

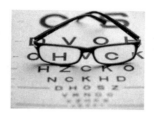

In the spring of 1985, for the first time I took part in a piano competition in Naples and I won it. I received a cash prize and my mom bought me a new pair of glasses.

It seemed like a harbinger of fate. Those glasses were a metaphor for a change.

My piano teacher Francesca one day repeated what Signora Giovanna had told me a few years earlier: "You'll soon have to leave here."

Francesca took me to Maria Pia in Naples. She told me that she was the teacher who could give an edge to my piano technique, refresh and expand my repertoire. She told me she lived alone with her elderly father who was always in bed and also warned me that she had a somewhat lunatic personality, but I needn't have worried about that.

Miss Maria Pia, as she wanted to be called, was a good pianist and teacher and was well known in Naples. She was quite short-sighted and a little neurotic, the latter detail I had already been told about and it didn't bother me so much. The thing I didn't like at all was another: she smoked like a chimney.

Her studio was perpetually immersed in a blanket of smoke that not even the two huge windows near the piano were able to disperse.

I had gone from Francesca's freesias to the pungent smell of tobacco and this too made me nauseous.

The place was somewhat dark, full of books, vinyl records scattered everywhere and contemporary art paintings on the walls. When I entered her studio, I didn't hear any background music but all the noise and the bustle of the city.

Continuing my piano studies with her was a very different leap forward in many ways.

Meanwhile an incredible coincidence made me believe that seeing ghosts in my piano teachers' studios was a kind of strange routine for me.

Signora Giovanna's studio was imbued with something ancient and mysterious, with the two invisible daughters and that maid who occasionally appeared behind the frosted glass. Francesca's was silent and melancholic, haunted by the ghost of Marcel Proust. Inside the domain of Signorina Maria Pia, I instead imagined Charles Bukowsky grappling with his cursed poems, desperately hammering on his typewriter and swearing in his heavy American accent, with an overflowing smoking ashtray by his side. I could almost hear the loud clacking of the typewriter keys.

Under the guidance of Miss Maria Pia, my playing began to acquire more passionate and tormented sounds with Beethoven, Liszt and Brahms.

Music was revealing its dark side.

I stayed with her for only a short time, I think a year or so. She had some health issues and decided to interrupt the lessons as she was put on some treatment plan. She notified my parents with a phone call and gave my mother the number of Beatrice, a piano and harmony teacher who lived in Naples as well, not very far from her.

"Antimo will be in safe hands with Beatrice".

The Fool

Walking joyfully into the world

I was fifteen and I had to learn to travel alone. My small town was about thirty kilometres away from Naples and my parents could not take me there for piano lessons. On the day of class, my mom used to make me two sandwiches for my return trip and always gave me two envelopes with money, one for the piano lesson and another for an emergency call from a public telephone, should I be in any trouble.
Very soon I managed to get by and quickly became an expert on local buses, national trains and the underground service around Naples.

Beatrice's studio was on the eighth floor of a modern building, up on a hill called *Vomero*.
My mum accompanied me to meet her the first time.
Beatrice was in her forties and the first thing I noticed when I saw her was that she looked quite dishevelled, with rather heavy and slightly smeared makeup.

It seemed she had just woken up after a night of debauchery.

My mum kept silent throughout the lesson, but when we got back she looked at me in the lift and burst out laughing. "Well, I wish you good luck, my son!"

But despite her witchy look, she was quite a good teacher.

Just as Dante's Beatrice lifted the poet's mind to heavenly joy, my teacher Beatrice enabled me to discover the magic of polyphony.

With her I explored the structure of harmony, the foundations of music with a look at the infinite combinatorial possibilities of sounds.

The study of harmony helped me understand the colours of music but also the mood, the direction, the light. My ears were delighted to listen to new music styles, so different from each other. Beatrice introduced me to a new musical world: from madrigals to string quartets, from Bach's fugues to Stravinsky's symphonic works.

Studying harmony for me was like stargazing.

"Do you see this card?" she asked me one day. "It's the *Fool*... a great card for you!" Beatrice had a passion for tarot cards, she also had photos of Indian holy men and gurus all over her studio. No ghosts to be glimpsed this time but a cloying smell of incense that permeated the whole room. The piano smelled of sandalwood.

"It's time to prepare you for a serious school, the Conservatory. I think you're ready to take the big leap" she told me one day.

I was growing up and learning. I read a lot of books, music theory and music composition manuals, I had to study harmony rules, somewhat abstract concepts and write pages of exercises that honestly didn't seem to have much relation to the practical side of music. Sometimes, after weeks of inhuman effort, my exercises turned out wrong. Beatrice corrected them with red scratches in my notebook and shook her head in denial when the mistakes were too trivial. I did feel frustrated sometimes but knew I shouldn't give up.

At the end of the lesson, she used to read me the tarot cards and when the cards were good it made me forget about all the failed homework.

On the train back home, I often looked at my hands. I thought about my life and future. Everything was a continuous surprise and by now I understood that I was destined for something beautiful.

At home I spent most of my time in the living room where my piano was. There was a large window from which I could see a long balcony. On that balcony every now and then a young girl, our neighbour's daughter, would stop and listen to me and look inquisitive. She would occasionally greet me and clap when she liked some piece I was playing.

My grandmother often came into the living room to clean up, and also gave me her opinions on the pieces I was studying. She didn't understand anything about music but managed to convey her appreciation in a very original way: *In my opinion you run too much when you play, you have to be more gentle on the piano!* or *This piece is my favourite!* were her most frequent comments.

My Maestro

The time had come to take the plunge, and the doors of the *Domenico Cimarosa* Conservatory in Avellino opened wide for me.

I passed the admission exam and another important chapter in my life began.

Beatrice had prepared the ground for me for one of the crucial moments of my piano career: meeting with my new teacher, the pianist Franz Nicolosi.

I was overjoyed. The new maestro was a famous concert pianist, one who recorded albums and played in major theatres around the world.

He was entirely different from my past teachers.

The others had taught me to play the piano, he taught me the essence of music.

"You have such a lovely hand that is quick, accurate and expressive. *But forget everything you've done so far*" he said, when he first heard me playing the piano.

Years of passion and new discoveries unfolded under the guidance of this amazing Maestro, who did not have excellent communication or teaching abilities.

However, he was a superb pianist.
I have stolen a lot of his tricks from him.

He would sit down at the piano and play rather than describing a certain musical genre, a phrase, or anything else. I paid close attention and learned just by listening to him.
"There's not much to discuss!" he frequently said, *"The only way you and I can understand each other is by playing!"*
With him I studied difficult pieces such as Rachmaninov's *Etudes Tableaux* and Concerto No. 2, Prokofiev's arduous Sonata No. 7, Balakirew's virtuosic *Islamey*, some pyrotechnic paraphrases for piano by Thalberg and many others.
My experience with him opened up new avenues for my musical interpretation and helped me become more conscious of how to create my own sound.

Simply by hearing him play the piano.

He taught me how to *perform* the silence, to use phrasing, to deal with technically challenging passages and lure my audience.
He was a great Maestro even when he got the notes wrong. Once I was on stage with him during a live radio broadcast. As I turned the pages for him and noticed that he made some mistakes, I saw he knew how to recover and carry on in an absolutely admirable and elegant way.

"No-one noticed. Don't be afraid of making mistakes, everyone makes mistakes, we're human! Don't worry if you mess up a passage, simply mess it up better!" he often said.

And he greeted me with a wink from backstage.

A bite of the Big Apple

When I was little my father often instructed me: *"Finish your studies and leave - go far away, as far as possible."*
Where was far away? What country was that? Would I have to stay there or could I come back? Would I meet people like me or will those from this far away country be far more special? What would tell me if I'd come far enough away or if I was still too close?
Was there a map of this far away country?

I graduated from the Conservatory of music and finished my studies at the age of nineteen with a great piano diploma. The first big chapter of my career had been written.
Now it was time to improve and aim higher and higher.
My next goal would have been a master's degree from the Juilliard school in New York, one of the leading music schools in the world.
I got ready for the audition and in the meantime warned my American relatives: I'm coming!!!

A good part of my mother's family lived in New York, there was her sister and many other aunts and uncles. Most of them lived in Long Island, not far from Manhattan.

I had previously been to the 'Big Apple' before, but returning there always made me dizzy.

My aunt Antonietta accompanied me to the audition. I remember that as soon as we left Penn Station in Manhattan I got so emotional that I almost fainted.

My uncle Andy, Aunt Antonietta's husband, told me a little story the day before the audition: "A young musician arrives in New York and wants to go to Carnegie Hall, but gets lost on the way and then asks a policeman: *Sorry Sir, how do I get to Carnegie Hall?* The policeman replies: Ah…well, practice, practice, practice and for sure you'll get there!"

A few days later they let me know that the audition went well and therefore they were ready to welcome me for the master's degree in piano at the Juilliard school.

Wow!

There was only one tiny yet huge detail: if I remember correctly, the cost for that course was around twenty-seven thousand dollars a year - for four years - and unfortunately there were no scholarships for me.

Too much money! My family could never afford such a large amount to support me.

I had to give up.

New York had made me dream and experience a moment of pure magic, but I had to come back down to earth.

I had touched the walls of one of the most famous music schools in the world with my own hands and had taken a bite out of the Big Apple, unfortunately without eating it all.

But it was a good lesson and I returned home happy and motivated.

Music wasn't such an easy thing: daily life didn't have stage lights and I understood that the road was long and the hard work daunting.
Meantime I needed to earn something.
I didn't mind performing in churches for weddings - and occasionally even funeral services, in little pubs and restaurants to make a bit extra, and I also started going around playing keyboards with my friend and fellow student Biagio, a true piano bar expert. We had fun.
The *serious* music we had studied didn't give too many employment opportunities. But I didn't give up and kept dreaming about my concerts around the world.
Meantime I was learning, no longer from school but from life itself.

Suddenly something changed.

The phone call

It was 1996, I was in my early twenties, I remember it was the end of October and the phone rang late at night.
That sound changed the course of my life.
It was my buddy Biagio.
"Listen, they're looking for a pianist to embark on cruise ships. Are you up for trying? I don't feel like going and I've already given this agency your number. Someone will call you in a bit. I'm confident you can do it, you can succeed!".
"What? I'm sorry, Biagio, but why don't you go? It sounds like a wonderful opportunity!"
"No, I can't. I can't stand ships, I get seasick. You go."

That was the beginning of one of my life's most incredible chapters.

The Dream

Pedes in mare ad sidera visus
Feet on the water and gaze at the stars

Everything I had ever wanted —travelling, new places to explore, concerts all over the world—seemed to be before my eyes now, as if in a giant group photo of all my fantasies.

The dream was coming true and I most definitely would not have gone back home for dinner to abandon my childhood flights of fancy.
I couldn't resist taking advantage of that opportunity, so I ventured out from my small hometown for the first time in my life.

The port of Venice was home to the first ship I had ever boarded.
Her name was *The Azur*.
It wasn't that big or particularly beautiful inside, as far as I can recall. It set off from Venice heading to Croatia, the Greek islands, and Turkey.
She glided gracefully on the waves, and we appeared to be a big family sailing on a yacht.

I felt happy being there even when the sea was rough, which it frequently was.

It had a capacity of about five hundred people, between passengers and staff. There were four bars, two restaurants, a small casino, a tiny disco and a swimming pool.

Everything was tiny on that ship, especially my cabin. I had to share the bathroom with my neighbour, it had an entrance door on my side and one on the side of the cabin next door. A curious thing that made me laugh when I first entered it.

I performed in a lounge bar that also served as a theatre in the evening and had a small dance floor that could be created by simply moving chairs and tables to one side to make some space for passengers to dance.

Because the passengers were from different countries, I rapidly learned how to play an international repertoire by sight-reading any requests. Occasionally I accompanied the ballet dancers, some jazz vocalists, the acrobats and even a magician. That onboard magician, a hopeless Hungarian who could never get a trick right, is the character I remember best from that ship.

Once, during one of his gala evening shows, the drape that a dove was meant to emerge from caught fire.

He told me behind the curtain, shortly before the show started, that it was a number that he had practised only a few times.

A table with lit candles was on the little stage to set the atmosphere and the mood. An edge of the drape touched one of the candles during a quite awkward scenic movement that would have made a dove appear. A small fire developed!

From behind the scenes, a few technicians leapt in to put out the fire.

Whilst the magician tried to catch the scared dove which, poor thing, was flapping frantically on the tiny stage; I continued to play the piano in an effort to salvage what could be saved. But it turned out to be quite grotesque.

Between laughter and screams a wave of *ooooohhhh!!!* erupted from the audience.

A surreal and very *Fellinian* scene.

I had so much fun and I still have lasting memories of that old ship. When the contract ended, I cried my eyes out.

But the adventure didn't quite end there.

Since then I've been on bigger and bigger ships. Real floating cities with thousands of people on board.

Not just.

I have also played the piano in beautiful five-star hotels. From Tuscany to Sicily, from Miami to Montecarlo, from Sardinia to Jordan.

I have an unforgettable recall of one in particular, for a story I will now tell you.

It was a stunning hotel on the Southern coast of Sicily, next to the Castle of Falconara, a magnificent 14th century mansion, and situated between the cities of Gela and Licata, in the province of Agrigento.

The hotel was gently nestled between rocks, flowers, the majestic castle and the vastness of the Mediterranean Sea. It looked like a precious gem with breath-taking views.

As soon as I settled into the hotel, I learned that the owner of this castle, to which the hotel was annexed, was known by all as the *Baron*, a mysterious aristocrat who lived alone in this mansion with his son, his butlers and servants.

It was the sweltering summer of 2009. Sicily experienced highs of above forty degrees Celsius during that season.

A large garden with a gazebo, tables, and sunbeds was just in front of the sea and the open-air restaurant was perched on the edge of it.

The piano sat in a corner of the restaurant.

In the late afternoon, when it started to cool off a little, the hotel's wealthy international guests crowded around the lawn, sipping elaborate aperitifs by the light of citronella torches, the ladies wore sophisticated jewels that stood out against their golden tans and the garden was bathed in an intense effluvium of lustful fragrancies, exotic essential oils and volatile chatter.

It was in this atmosphere that I began to play the piano while a gigantic sun set grandly behind the castle.

That place was a great inspiration for me and I often liked to start my piano set with some music by Michel Legrand, Nino Rota, Philip Glass, Ludovico Einaudi, Ryuichi Sakamoto, Michael Nyman, Bill Evans on whose themes I loved to improvise.

In such an environment I felt like being part of a script for some film.

At dusk, the son of the Baron, the dreaded and mysterious owner, descended from that castle. This young man in his thirties completely embodied the stereotype of the decadent lord, one of those figures from Giuseppe Tomasi di Lampedusa's classic *The Leopard.*

He had a fairly evident physical disability: a limp.

He was clearly visible from afar as he strode down the cobbled street with his cane and swinging gait. He sat at the tables near the piano and in a flash the waiters raced over to serve him.

Like an owl on a perch, the Baron's son observed everything and everyone.

Rumour had it that he was always alone and desperately hunting for a wife, but had no luck. As days went by in that scorching summer, consecutive and increasingly detailed information about the lonely aristocrat in search of a soul mate was provided on regular basis in the staff cafeteria. This issue fuelled the mystery around his character and filled the air with a fairytale feel.

In the hotel, there were some really pretty housekeepers. Among them was Roberta. A brunette with very delicate features and always smiling. She often asked me to play her a piece by Morricone when she happened to pass by the piano.

And so the days went by slowly and it seemed to me that I was living in a kind of dream from which I could not wake up. It seemed that nobody really cared about time.

I had most of the days entirely for myself, as I was starting work late in the afternoon, so I would occasionally go out with my car and drive around looking for new places to discover.

I went to see *Valle dei Templi* – the Valley of the Temples – in Agrigento, undoubtedly the most important vestige of the Hellenic classical culture in Sicily.

I visited Piazza Armerina, home to the beautiful Roman *Villa del Casale* and its famous mosaics, described as the finest ones in the Roman world. Among them are the *Bikini Girls*, which portray young women performing sports dressed in what look like the first bikinis of human history.

Then I visited Caltagirone, where I came across some wonderful hand-crafted works of art, in particular the *Moor's Heads*.

The Moor's Head is a characteristic object of the Sicilian tradition. It is a very beautifully hand-painted ceramic vase used as an ornament, depicting the face of a Moor, usually alongside that of a young woman.

I learned about the incredible story behind it. An ancient legend narrates that around the year 1100, during the period of the domination of the Moors in Sicily, in the *Kalsa* district of Palermo, there had lived a beautiful girl. This girl was always at home, and spent her days taking care of the plants on her balcony. One day a young and handsome Moor walked past her balcony, looked up and immediately fell in love with her.

Without much further ado he hurried up the steps, entered the girl's house and declared his love for her. The girl, struck by so much ardour, reciprocated the love of the young Moor. But her happiness vanished as she subsequently learned that her beloved would soon leave her to return to the East, where a wife awaited him.

Hurt by so much pain, one night the girl waited for the Moor to fall asleep in her arms and cut his head off.

She made a vase of the Moor's head and planted basil inside, then put it on display outside her balcony.

In this way, the Moor, unable to leave anymore, would remain with her forever.

Oh, how I loved Sicily! All around me was mystery, passion, love, pain.
Sicily's beauty, history, and natural wonders captivated me no end.

Back at the hotel where I was working, one day I caught a glimpse of Roberta the pretty housekeeper, sitting alone in a corner in the staff cafeteria. She looked very serious and sad, almost unrecognisable.
"Roberta, how are you doing?"
"I'm anxious. Recently, I got a message that disturbed me."
"Can I help you in any way?"
"The Baron's son has invited me to the castle and I don't know whether to go. I'm undecided."
"Wow, it sounds like something from a fairytale!"
"Yes, but…he writes me in the letter that he's in love with me. But I don't like him, he's not my type. I don't want to go there!"
"I see…"

A few days later, I found out that Roberta had chosen to trust her gut instinct. She did not accept the invitation to go to the castle.

The days dragged very slowly under that blazing sun. I frequently spent the mornings at the beach or walking near the castle.
I never again saw the Baron's son. I imagined him segregated in his castle, hurt by the same pain the legendary beautiful maiden had felt for the unfaithful Moor, smashing priceless objects scattered throughout the rooms with his cane, giving vent to his anger at having received a refusal from the beautiful Roberta.

I had reached the end of my contract in that incredible place and it was time for me to leave.
I will never forget that long, hot Sicilian summer of 2009.

Between ships and hotels, I've seen wonderful places and met incredible people.
I was overjoyed, taking pictures everywhere, writing my travel journal.

The *souks* of Casablanca, the spices of Istanbul, the colours of Alexandria, the seduction of Sicily, the light of Marseilles. I daydreamed on the Baltic, I saw euphoric dolphins jumping in the waves for miles off Gibraltar, I've heard incredible stories from total strangers, watched the Stromboli volcano erupt at close range, enjoyed the most spectacular fireworks in Madeira, got terrified during hurricanes on the high seas and cried in front of breathtaking sunsets.

The wind of life was blowing hard in my face.
But above all to the sea, to that incredible blue mass, with its incessant breath, I entrusted my words, dreams, fears. Its perennial movement was for me the very meaning of life.
It was music and that music took me around the world.
It was my dream and I was living it.

Disaster

*Derived from the Latin suffix **dis** (disintegration, separation) and*
***astro** (star), it was used to name stellar cataclysms.*
By extension, a bad star.

In 2012 I was working as resident pianist aboard the Costa Concordia cruise ship. A colossal seventeen-deck ship that could carry up to about five thousand people, including passengers and crew. There were five restaurants, some thirteen lounge bars, a casino, four swimming pools, a magnificent theatre, a large Wellness centre and all possible on-board comforts and amenities.
It was January 13th, 2012. The ship had left the port of Civitavecchia, known as *Port of Rome* at 7.30 pm heading to Savona, north-west Italy.
I was playing in a bar called Bar Vienna, located on the fifth deck, near the stern of the ship.
There was a bunch of well-dressed passengers scattered all around this beautiful room.

Low lights, soft chatter, glittering jewels, clinking glasses, musky vanilla, tuberose and sandalwood accords of sophisticated *eaux de parfums*.
All so cinematic.
My stage partners were a trio of Hungarian musicians. We took turns and had slots of forty-five minute shifts each.
The trio leader Sandor, a huge gypsy from Budapest who played the violin like a demon, told me he was going to take a nap in the cabin during the break. He was feeling a bit unwell - we would meet again later on. "Of course Sandor, enjoy your break!"

At 9.30 pm I jumped on stage where my Yamaha piano was waiting for me.
It was just such a beautiful evening. I peered through the portholes of the bar as I played. The sea was calm and the stars twinkled in the sky like Christmas lights.
My fingers flew over the piano like wings of a dream.
I was completely immersed in my beautiful routine.

I had just started playing one of my own compositions when the ship suddenly started tilting. It was 9.42 pm.
The piano was torn from its safety locks and began to swing across the stage.
I fell off my chair.

... *a scary scene!*

Passengers began to flee in all directions.

I couldn't give myself any explanation about this. The sea was calm, the weather conditions were perfect. Why was the ship suddenly tilting?

Later on, I learned that the Concordia was navigating in quite shallow waters off the coast of the beautiful Isola del Giglio, in Tuscany.

At about 9.45 pm the port side of the ship struck a submerged rock.

There was a terrifying roar as plates and glasses flew and crashed into the packed bars and restaurants.

Panic set in.

The impact with the rock caused a lengthy gash on the side of the ship, a wound about seventy metres long.

An absurd accident.

Chaos erupted.

The ship was taking on more and more water and was leaning to one side.

We were in the middle of a shipwreck.

The general emergency signal was sounded and much later, the captain finally ordered us to abandon ship.

Our crew cabins were all on deck zero. I thought about the things I'd left there, all my papers, my books. I wanted to go down from the fifth deck to check it and eventually take some of my belongings but the water was rapidly flooding the lower side of the ship - just where my cabin was.

I had a sudden thought and felt my blood freeze: *my colleague Sandor was downstairs in his cabin.*
I was worried about him.

Meanwhile the ship leaned over more and more.

I put on my life vest, reached my emergency muster station and followed all the instructions from my safety booklet.
The 'Abandon Ship' signal was sent after quite some time, but no-one from the bridge or any safety officer came to get me.
I didn't know how to escape from there.
The Concordia was tilting and sinking and my life raft was already under water.
Apparently I was pretty much without hope.
It was time to take action.
I climbed up some railings, pipes, metal parts of the ship and through a broken embarkation gate. After a while I found myself on the wounded flank of the Concordia, hanging by a cable and waiting for help.

The ship looked like a giant, mortally wounded whale and I was on top of it.
After about six excruciating hours, I was spotted from a helicopter and ultimately rescued.

My colleague Sandor had promised me that we would meet again in my break.

I never saw him again.

Just as I never saw another colleague of mine again. Giuseppe, the drummer of the main band who worked in the Grand Bar Berlin, the largest bar on the ship.

That accident claimed the lives of thirty-two people.

I often think that it could have happened to me if I hadn't been in that bar playing the piano.

Music had just saved my life.

I returned home. All I had left was my phone, a pen and my ship crew member ID. I took it from my pocket, the photo was almost completely faded. I dropped out of the picture.

At the doorway stood my father and mother in tears.

Post Traumatic Stress Disorder

As an alternative to benzodiazepines, in moderate anxiety natural remedies can be used, for example supplements such as melissa, hawthorn, passionflower, linden, lavender. However, for moderate insomnia, your doctor may prescribe you a hypnotic for a few days. In chronic insomnia, lasting more than four weeks, a treatment with an antidepressant is preferable. In any case, to prevent any addiction it is better to use hypnotic drugs for the shortest possible time, at the lowest dose.

A heavy curtain fell on one the most incredible chapters of my life.

After that terrible accident, many things have changed.
The ghosts and the voices of that tragic night have haunted me for years. I could still hear that horrifying polyphony of pain.

I had become an insomniac, easy prey to anxiety and depression.

"You suffer from Post Traumatic Stress Disorder. These might make you feel a little better."
The doctor introduced me to a number of medicines. They had strange names: Benzodiazepines...Xanax...Rohypnol... Tavor.
"Post Traumatic Stress Disorder?"
"What's that??"
"PTSD is a discomfort that develops when witnessing traumatic events, also widespread among soldiers returning from wars. It will take some time before you get rid of it, that's why I have recommended these pills to you."

This condition gradually became a silent monster stirring inside me, leaving me at the mercy of sudden anxiety attacks, sleepless nights, and a constant restlessness in my body and spirit.
All the sights and sounds of that night on the Concordia came back in time to find me and hunt me down. I felt like a deer scurrying through the snow hunted by hungry wolves. Really, *really* hard to escape.
I could no longer find peace, I was no longer interacting with my family and I had reduced contact with my friends to almost zero.
But still I decided not to take those medicines with those strange names. I had to find a different solution. I never liked medicines and I was afraid of them. I feared they might make me lose control and screw up my head, destroy my sense of Self, my memories and leave me half-dazed on the edge of my life.

I had to do it by myself.
I had to change something, but I didn't know what.
I had very little energy but slowly an idea began to dawn.
My life was at a turning point.

After years spent around the world playing the piano, the time had come to close this chapter, leave for a different destination and start again from scratch.
That shipwreck had also been a metaphorical representation of my own personal shipwreck but I had hope, I had to emerge and breathe, be reborn.

Away from my country, far from everything and everyone.

London

Go to great lengths in pursuit of a story

So, I did the maths: I was in my early forties, in a desperate condition: no job, I hadn't been compensated after that scary accident, my private life was a mess and I was on the verge of a nervous breakdown.

I dropped everything and with the very little money I had scraped together by selling my beloved piano, I moved to London, a place where no one knew me.

I had been to London on holiday for a week a few years before, but only remembered the touristic areas.

This time I had a different motivation. I went there to find purpose in my life.

I rented a room in Peckham, south of the Thames, not far from Greenwich.

It was always cold in that house. There were other roommates: two brothers and a couple with a baby daughter whose father was the owner. All of them Lithuanians.

I often argued with the owner, that bastard turned off the heat at night to save on bills. I had also bought a second-hand bicycle that he occasionally took without asking my permission.
I spent whole days sitting on my bed looking for work, any job. The Wi-Fi at the house was quite weak and so I sometimes went to the nearby McDonald's. The coffee was horrible but the connection there was good.

Looking for a way out, I was in a terrible situation.

Peckham reminded me of southern Italy, where I come from. A multi-ethnic neighbourhood, vibrant and colourful, reputed to be quite a dodgy area in the recent past.
I loved strolling up and down Rye Lane, the main street, a concentrate of incredible exoticism, it looked like a caravan oasis that made me dizzy: spices, fabrics, wig shops, Afghani, Kurdish, Lebanese food, Vietnamese, Hispanic, Irish butchers, halal food stalls, a Chinese supermarket with small sharks and never seen before fish in the tank, carpets, beggars, African hairdressers open day and night, all type of

smells coming from who knows where, makeshift places of worship in rundown warehouses, graffiti, Indian shops with unimaginable interiors, charity shops where I bought my first head-to-toe outfit for less than ten pounds.

If the rest of the world shut down, you'd find everything you need to live in Peckham.

I read an advertisement for a job in Notting Hill in a vinyl shop. I went for the interview. They were looking for someone with some cultural background in music. Could do for me maybe.

It was a shop with a creaky wooden floor and a strong smell of old artefacts.

A heavily tattooed guy handed me a questionnaire.

How did Marvin Gaye die?

How many records have Fleetwood Mac sold?

Do you remember the names of Deep Purple's members?

And other similar questions.

The test went wrong and I didn't get the job.

Okay. We change direction.

Again looking for a job in newspapers and websites.

This time the change had to be radical.

The classic position of waiter seemed like a last resort.

The Victoria and Albert museum

A company was looking for waiters even with zero experience, but I prepared a brand new curriculum, quite appealing and catchy, just to be on the safe side. I shouldn't and couldn't waste time. I needed money.

In my CV, I had worked in the coolest bars and restaurants in New York and Miami.

Lies.

The interview went well and I got the job. This company had bars and restaurants in London's most famous museums.

I was sent to the Victoria and Albert Museum's restaurant, in South Kensington, one day in March 2013.

White shirt, black trousers, black shoes. I wrote the name of the restaurant manager on a piece of paper.

I stuffed everything into my rucksack and went to catch the 345 bus from Peckham to South Kensington. The appointment was at nine in the morning.

The 345 crossed a large part of the area south of the Thames, the working-class districts of Peckham, Camberwell, Brixton,

Stockwell and then went up past Battersea, towards richer areas such as Chelsea and South Kensington.

As the bus cut through these areas from South East to West London, I couldn't help but notice the variety and diversity of passengers. The sounds, the languages, the expressions, the facial features mutated as the bus went along. *It was like browsing through a beauty atlas.* Utterly fascinating.

Around Peckham the bus carried mainly passengers of African origin, towards Brixton Jamaicans, Brazilians and generally South Americans, around Stockwell there were many Portuguese and Eastern Europeans and towards the end of the bus route I was almost alone.

The 345 last stop was the Natural History Museum, right next to the Victoria and Albert museum.

When I got off the bus, I was surprised by the grandeur of this elaborate gothic architecture that dominated the busy Cromwell Road. Two huge castles that my eyes could hardly contain.

On the main entrance door of the V&A I read: *The excellence of every art must consist in the complete accomplishment of its purpose.*

Well, I said to myself. I don't know why but, even though I was there for a job as a waiter, this sentence encouraged me. It seemed that I was there for a reason that went far beyond that job and that I was not yet aware of.

The Victoria and Albert museum indeed took me by surprise. The long corridors, the huge rooms full of marbles, busts, statues, tapestries and pieces from every corner of the world made me slightly dizzy.

What a marvellous place!

A new adventure

That day I didn't have much spirit to appreciate all those museum wonders as I was a little anxious about this new chapter of my life. I found myself in a room with other aspiring waiters like me, quickly got changed and introduced myself to the manager who asked me to follow him.

From the locker room he took me to the museum's historical café, where the restaurant was, my new workplace.

The restaurant had four main sections: coffee, dessert, hot and cold food. They were all along the main large corridor at the rear of the museum.

Most of the tables were spread out behind the bar, in three quite beautiful rooms.

In the centre was the Gamble Room, to each side the Morris and Poynter rooms.

I was introduced to a sinuous French guy. His figure reminded me of bicycle bells emerging from milky mists in the countryside. He repeatedly rubbed his red runny nose with his arm and sniffled immediately after.

He was in the largest hall, the Gamble room, entrenched behind a dark, greasy wooden counter. There were various types of containers and a big trolley.

"This is the room" - the manager said – "and this guy is your fellow team member who will tell you what to do. Have a nice day."

'There is nothing better for a man than he should eat and drink, and make his soul enjoy good in his labour.' It was written high up on the large majolica tiles arranged along the semi-circular walls of the Gamble room. Later on, I learned this sentence was an excerpt from Ecclesiastes in the Bible.

The French guy's name was Benoit. He sounded quite strange. His English seemed to be secluded deep in his mouth, like behind a barricade, bent over underground murmured vowels blown by a light wind of breath that smelled of broth.

He spoke little and never smiled.
I barely understood the directives:
"Throw it there and this never goes here" or *"When the trolley is full you have to take it over there!"*
This character appeared to me like a photo taken against his will, an asymmetry in his look, his body tilting whilst wiping a tray and his quick peek that mechanically drew a triangle between the tray, the room and my figure.
Benoit seemed like he was being manoeuvred by a grumpy puppet master.
As a child I guess he would spend his summer at sea under a parasol rather than jumping with his friends in the waves.

The air was dense and saturated with ever-expanding chaotic chatter, sound waves mixing up with the thick and cloying smell of food. I felt a bit queasy.

It was lunch time and the museum's cafe was quite busy.

With a detached nonchalance Benoit delved his hands in a mishmash of bones, skins, fish scales, bitten bread, mugs with lipstick traces, broth and other types of slurry material of different texture, density and colour.

Clearly this man was undisturbed and imperturbable. To him it was probably just like a Sunday walk in the city sewer.

On my first day the French guy immediately made me understand that he didn't give a damn about me.

"Break time!" he said and vanished in the noisy crowd, leaving me there, behind that greasy counter, on my own.

It was quite clear to me now.

Needless to ask how I got to that point.

I stood for a moment watching everything and everyone from behind that wooden trench.

There was a mirror behind me: I tried several times to look at myself but couldn't see any reflection of my image in it. I felt like I was made up of all the chaos I was being exposed to in the room and I thought that the mirror was just reflecting my own cacophony, the deafening dissonance of my thoughts.

Before my mind lined up all the ducks, I noticed other fellow team members approaching with trays and tired faces.

They looked like celebrants in a procession with votive offerings, their expression charged with the symbolic weight of a ritual.

In no time I was submerged by dirty dishes, screeching sounds, novel odours, leftovers and different kinds of waste.

So, after surviving a shipwreck and a period of long unemployment, I became a waiter at the prestigious V&A Museum cafe in South Kensington, London.

That first, intense day of work ended up on a bench, with a cigarette, legs and back in pieces and a few words exchanged with other fellow waiters whose names were totally unknown to me.
We were mostly silent and looked like war veterans waiting for the Red Cross.

The 345 bus took me slowly back home and, as it crossed the city, I had the impression that it was traversing my own mind, from side to side.

Another adventure had begun.

The ball is in your court

My days all looked the same: early in the morning I was in charge of preparing the *floor* of the museum restaurant together with other sleepy waiters. There were heavy tables and hundreds of chairs to be quickly arranged, cakes, sandwiches and all the food to be displayed on the counter and in the fridges.

But there was something that silently illuminated the darkness in my soul.

In the room where I worked there was a piano and I polished that piano every day.

Every now and then someone came to play it. They told me he was a young student at the Royal College of Music, one of the most important music schools in the world, a stone's throw from the museum.

This young pianist especially liked Beethoven and Brahms.

"Excuse me Maestro, can I clean the piano before you start playing?"

"Sure. Go ahead."

This guy had a very long beard. He was Greek and always had a frown on his face.

And I was cleaning that piano instead of playing it!

My nights became longer and longer and more tormented my waking states. In my mind I projected images of me playing around the world and people smiling at me.

I had to do something. I had to change something.

A couple of months went by: I had pain all over my body. My back was practically broken, my legs and hands aching, but I went on as if in a state of hypnosis.

I finally got up the courage to talk to the manager.

"Excuse me, I have a request to make."

"Tell me?"

"Can I play that piano?"

"What? What's your name?"

"My name is Antimo, I'm a pianist!"

"We already have one who comes every week to play!"

"I know Sir, I'm just asking you to let me have a turn on that piano?"

"Okay, our resident pianist isn't coming tomorrow. Finish your shift, present yourself well and show me how good you are!"

"Thanks a lot, Sir."

I cried that day on the 345 bus.

The next day I was very nervous at work and I dropped and smashed a couple of plates and glasses.

I finished my shift, went to the locker room and changed quickly.

I was ready but quite anxious. I hadn't touched a piano in months.

How would it go?

It was nearly three in the afternoon on April 1, 2013. The Gamble Room was busy.

I sat down at the piano, a Kawai, old but in good condition.

I wasn't sure what to do, so I started improvising.

I had listened to the other pianist several times and I already knew that the piano sound was a bit metallic, but I liked it.

Slowly my hands awoke from a long sleep. At first it all seemed and sounded new to me, as if I had never played a piano before in my life.

I was smiling. My body was warming up.

Music was emerging from unfathomable depths to be with me again.

An invisible harmony spread in the air and changed things around me. Everything took on new forms, objects, people, the air itself, that time of the day, the light, the weather outside, and it seemed that everything was mine.

Hello everyone, my name is Antimo, you don't know me …

The piano was in the centre of the magnificent Gamble Room.

They were sitting all around me, I felt their breath, I felt their lives close to mine.

The first applause erupted in the air like a little explosion of joy.

My forehead shone with sweat.

My manager was watching me from a distance. I could not interpret his expression. His gaze worried me a little. I was afraid at first that maybe he didn't like my music.

I continued playing a second piece, still improvising, at the end of which a lady came up and left a £10 tip on the piano.

74

She made a coquettish little bounce on her high heels and said: "Lovely music!"

"Could you please see me in my office?" my manager asked me.

"We received quite positive feedback from our visitors about your performance, well done. But why didn't you tell me right away that you were a pianist, why did you write in your CV that you're a waiter and not a musician?"

"It's a long story, Sir. Playing the piano is what I've been doing all my life, it has always been my passion and my job, but I had a very traumatic experience recently. I survived a terrible accident and couldn't play anymore. I tried to forget about my beautiful life of travelling the world playing music and decided to start from scratch in London with another job. But then I bumped into that piano and decided to give it another try..."

"Wow, what story is this? Ok, let me propose something to you. You stay with us working in the morning as a waiter and I'll give you one day a week in the afternoon as a pianist. What do you say?"

"It sounds great!"

Waiter and Pianist

It was the spring of 2013, the days at the piano became two, then three, then four.
Within a few weeks I became the museum's pianist-in-residence, but ... in the mornings I always worked as a waiter.

After that accident on the ship, I had lost everything and received no financial compensation. I had very little money and a room in shared accommodation in London cost me about seven hundred pounds per month.

My work shift as a waiter began at 9 am and ended at 2.30 pm, then I quickly got changed in the dressing room to begin the piano shift from 3 to 5 pm.

I no longer felt the fatigue of moving marble tables around, rearranging hundreds of chairs, cleaning trays and pushing trolleys full of leftovers and rubbish. The hours spent working as a waiter went by quickly and I couldn't wait to get my hands, even if a little peeled and damaged, on that piano. It was all so weird!

In my imagination I looked like Clark Kent quickly changing in the phone booth into Superman for some important mission.
"Dreams save us, dreams lift us up and transform us" the super-hero used to say.
Over time I was pretty much sure that this was my mission: to play the piano and share my emotions with the world.
I was on a mission to save my life as well, to forget about that traumatic accident on the ship, to hope, to be able to sleep peacefully with no ghosts haunting my mind.
Music had become the best form of self-therapy to overcome that nightmare.

I was forty-two and my second life had just begun.

I also got back to my writing, my other great passion after music.
I needed to release my tension, so I started gathering what was left of me and remembering what had happened to me. A way to empty myself and move on.

I wrote a book entitled *The Pianist of Concordia,* a collection of memories and stories from when I was on that ship, first in Italian, then released in English.
At that time, writing became as vital to me as playing.
I was alone with my words and my music.

And then living that life in an unknown, immense, chaotic, fast-paced, incredibly cosmopolitan and beautiful city like London, made me want to document this new adventure. I wanted to treasure the memory of it all.
I had taken the challenging and daring decision to leave my country, to depart immediately, forgetting about my past and starting from scratch in a new city. Then a miracle occurred when I discovered a piano in the same beautiful museum where I was employed as a waiter.
An incredible synchronicity.

When I looked at it from afar, that Kawai piano seemed absorbed in studious reflection.
It seemed to be reflecting on me, on us all, indeed! *"I'm here for you, man"* it seemed to whisper to me.
The image of that piano with its lid open reminded me of a sailing boat.
Suddenly I dreamed of going back to playing around the world. I was on the high and wavy seas at the helm of my beloved sailing piano.
We had sailed the seven seas to discover the world and now we were there, docked in the port of that magnificent museum.
Even the shape of the Gamble Room reminded me of a cove, a quiet gulf sheltered from the storms of my past.
It was the world coming to visit US now. We had so many stories to tell and wanted to hear from others.

Meantime I started saving some money and after a few months I finally managed to buy an electronic piano. I had also moved to another flat, still in the Peckham area. My new piano was placed in a corner of my new tiny room.

I needed to practise and compose new music. The inspiration gradually came to find me.

At the beginning of my new adventure as a waiter and pianist, everything happened to me.

My face and my story began to be quite popular among the visitors at the Victoria and Albert Museum and so my presence there aroused much curiosity.

Who was this guy?

In the morning sometimes I would serve coffee or food to the same people who would then ask me what time I would start playing the piano in the afternoon.

Sometimes I worked at the restaurant till and together with the receipt I handed my flyers to customers with the times of my gigs at the V&A.

A lady once came to say hello after my piano performance and said to me:

"You have a familiar face, sorry to tell you but you look very much like a waiter who served us that salmon and salad this morning".

"Dear lady, it's precisely me myself!"

Stories and People at the Museum

"You see" - my friend Alex said once — *"when you play you shoot an arrow into the air. This may pierce someone's heart, causing a kind of wound. The wounded one goes in search of the bow where the arrow started from and can't help but come in your direction".*

I have incredible stories in my heart, lots of notebooks filled with precious memories. Since 2013 many people who visited the museum and approached me left their mark: messages in various languages, poems, books, gifts, children's drawings and portraits of me left on the piano.
Not only tourists, but also locals, who have been listening to me playing at the V&A for years on regular basis.

I will never forget that girl who came up one rainy October afternoon, crying and telling me that, because of my music, she had stayed too long at the museum and had forgotten to get back to the station in time to catch the last bus back to the north of England.

And Amanda, the elderly Greek lady who always came with her partner Peter on Fridays, for the late opening of the museum.

Her routine was buying food at the museum restaurant and coming to me at the piano to say hello with a kiss on my forehead:

"You, because of your name, remind me of my beloved homeland, Greece, Onassis, Maria Callas, Theodorakis. But I love Italy, Mastroianni, Sophia Loren, Fellini..." She had a way of gesturing with her slender arms that seemed to help her retrieve her past, as if she were rowing in a river and her memories were all in the wake of her boat.

Then she would say something in Greek that I've never understood and she's never translated for me in the almost ten years that I've known her. Then as she returned to the table where her Peter was sitting, she asked everyone in the room to listen to me carefully with that look of a caring and a little grumpy Grandma.

"This guy is called Antimo, he's got a Greek name but he is Italian. You'd better listen carefully to his music!"

Oh Amanda, what a character!

Patricia and Anne, two flight attendants working for an American airline, came to listen to me every time they flew into London from who knows where. Every time I saw them they told me about their family, their children growing up, the political situation in America, as well as the best place to eat in Puerto Vallarta, Mexico or somewhere else in the world. Listening to them was like travelling around the planet without moving from that coffee table.

They were always in good spirits, like straight out of a Broadway show, and their arrival was always anticipated by a glass of Merlot handed to me on the piano. When that glass of red wine finally appeared, I turned to look around and just a moment later their loud 'Hellooooo' rang out along with their gorgeous and flashing American billboard smile, followed by a vigorous, tight hug.

We resumed speeches or life stories made months before as if time had never passed.

"And now play us our favourite song!"

They vanished noisily in the afternoon always leaving a smile on my face.

"See you soon, baby!"

I remember a mysterious lady who occasionally came to visit, dressed like Audrey Hepburn, the protagonist of *Breakfast at Tiffany's*. She always wore flamboyant, sophisticated pastel-coloured clothes, came to the piano and slipped a £20 note in the middle of my sheet music book.

"Thank you for the music".

Her face was concealed under her hat's wide brim, so I was never able to see it.

She left a trail of thick, alluring scent of intoxicating, creamy white flowers.

After the museum visit, I suppose she would have made a cameo appearance in a film or in some Scott Fitzgerald book. For some time, I thought that lady was a figment of my imagination.

Kate and Angela were two funny transvestites, a bit shabby and aged, who came on Saturday afternoons. They crossed the room smiling, swaying and rocking a little on their heels, eventually collapsing on the large bench of the Gamble Room. Exhausted by the effort of balancing their gait, their smiles often turned into grimaces of pain, as if all that pantomime had come at a high price.

They usually had a classic Earl Grey tea with scones and clotted cream and waved at me from afar.
"Hello Darling, lovely to see you!"
Kate always wore colourful hats with bright little flowers, Angela had incipient baldness which, over the years, uncovered a lot of her skull and sometimes she even showed up with a devil-may-care 3-day beard.
Only years later I was told that their real names were Ian and Michael.
A lovely couple!

One day at the museum I met Ruth, an American lady from New Jersey.
She listened to my music, offered me a glass of wine and we started talking. I told her my story about the shipwreck and she was very moved.
She went away and told me that we would meet again sooner or later.

A few days later I received a call from the BBC. Someone had written a letter to a producer asking to grant me an interview and tell my story. It had obviously been Ruth.

I have been to the BBC radio and TV studios several times. My story was also covered in the Times and many other newspapers.
I was greatly touched by Ruth's kindness and wrote her a long letter of gratitude.

Israel, a Spanish professor of English literature from Madrid came to the museum every summer.
I had previously met him at the museum on July 27th, 2017, my birthday. I saw him again on July 27th of the following year. I immediately thought of the strange coincidence, but I would not have expected him to remember it.
I saw him in the crowd and went to greet him during one of my breaks.
"*Hola* Israel, great to see you again! How are you?"
After a good chat, I said goodbye and went to the bathroom before resuming my playing.

That afternoon the museum was rather busy and the Gamble Room was full.

Upon returning from the bathroom, I noticed that there was a lady sitting at the piano waiting for me.

What was this lady doing in my place?

At a sign from Israel this lady started playing and the whole room joined in chorus to sing *Happy Birthday to You*.

This brought me to tears actually. Come to think of it, no one had ever played that little song to me on the piano on my birthday. I was overjoyed!

Whilst I was in the bathroom, Israel had a chat with a lady sitting near his table. The lady was a pianist and he asked her to play the birthday song for me. He had organised everything in just a few minutes.

Not only did Israel remember my birthday, he also conjured me up a surprise that I will never forget.

I have met people who are still in my life and sadly I have lost touch with others as well.

I've played for them, at their weddings, at their parties, I've dedicated to them my music, I've listened to their stories, I've cried and laughed with them, I've taught them a little piano and sometime sadly bade them farewell in church.

Music has opened up new worlds to me, it has drawn to me a humanity that I would have never expected.

After a terrible trauma, it gave me my life back.

I kept my job as a waiter for a couple more years and then, when my financial situation was a little more stable, I hung up my apron and devoted myself solely to my job as Pianist in Residence at the Victoria and Albert Museum.

Inner Landscape

Meanwhile, I felt the urge to compose new music. My new life didn't completely force my past into a corner. The memory of the dreadful night was still lingering upon the aftermath of that accident and I wanted to exorcise it.

Apart from journalling, I needed something more powerful and music came to see me again.

I had a dream, to pay a tribute to the victims of that shipwreck, those thirty-two people who were with me that night on that cursed ship and with a twist of fate, lost their lives.

A project began to dawn. I called it **Inner Landscape**.

Even though I was now living in a metropolis with millions of people around me, immediately after the accident I withdrew into myself, into the quiet retreat of my silent room. I imagined opening a window inwards. I wanted to map the emotional geography of my inner landscape, picking up the broken pieces of my life, in the attempt to reconstruct the mosaic of my world, my image, the memory of myself.

And above all, to take a closer look into the darkness of that fateful night, when my dreams fell from grace.

I had decided to change my life and start from scratch in London. It all happened very quickly and this also helped me to distract myself and not think about the ghosts of that night.

But I wanted to call them back, confront them and annihilate them.

Remembering was important. Recalling the moments, the last lived on that ship, to exorcise, rebuild and move forward.

From that open window, a new light was cast onto the bowels of that night.

So I started the **Inner Landscape** project.

The images turned into notes, what I had seen that night became music under my fingers.

Where is everybody? is one of the first pieces I wrote for this project. It reflects my thoughts during my escape from the ship, when I hung by a hawser on the flank of the sinking Concordia. Alone under that starry sky, I thought about the absurdity of that accident and how quickly the happy and carefree atmosphere of that cruise had turned into pain and tragedy.

Where were my travel companions? Where had they gone?

I wanted my music to be my voice, to call out and find them, to reassure me that they were still alive and that everything would soon be back to normal.

The piece *'Seven short blasts and one long'* is an escalation of tension that culminates with the nefarious seven short blasts and one longer one, the general emergency signal on ships. That distress signal, the sound of those apocalyptic sirens ripping through the night, was the beginning of the nightmare. I wanted to reproduce the disturbing effect of that alarm by using the low bass sound of the piano, marked heavily by the left hand.

Unfortunately that accident created its victims and this inspired one of the most touching pieces of this album, which is also the simplest of all. It is called *Thirty-two*, whose main melody is made up of thirty-two notes. Every single note is a tribute to the memory of every single victim of that shipwreck.

The Inner Landscape project ended with a great liberating cry. Ten piano pieces that cost me a LOT to write in terms of emotions. But I immediately felt better from the cathartic effect the project had on me. My music was chasing away the ghosts of that night and it turned out to be the best substitute for those medicines to treat my PTSD.

I had a great desire to play in public. I wanted these pieces to be heard, I wanted to tell my story through my music.
A public concert was the only way to break the ice.
But would anyone come? I wasn't really known here in London.
I decided to take the leap. *I could certainly do something!*
I had saved up some money with my job as a waiter and started looking for a venue to hire for my concert.

After a long search I found a very beautiful church, St. Giles in the Fields - the *Poets' Church*, with Palladian architecture and a hundred-year-old *Bechstein* piano in quite good condition and with a beautiful resonance.

The church was right in the heart of London, between Charing Cross, Tottenham Court Road and minutes away from Soho. It seemed to me strategically positioned.

Well, now it was time to get someone to come and hear me, so I started a promotional campaign for my concert, printing flyers and distributing them around, telling everyone I knew about it.

The day finally arrived. It was September the 12th, 2015.

I had pretty much taken care of all the details of the event myself. Some of my collaborators were fellow waiters at the Victoria and Albert Museum. So I had two girls at the door to check tickets, someone in the hall for the lights and another friend handing out the programme leaflets.

It was my first concert in London and my first performance of the entire **Inner Landscape** album.

I was on Cloud Nine!

When the lights went out and I walked from backstage to the piano, I saw nothing, my vision was blurred.

I finished my first piece and the first round of applause burst.

I turned to the audience, there were faces I knew and some I didn't.

The church was full as much as my heart filled up with joy.

The last piece was *Thirty-two*, the one I had dedicated to the thirty-two victims of the shipwreck. The simple notes of the melody stretched out one after the other. In between there was a deep silence, which enveloped the whole church, as in a slow ceremonial of commemoration.

I was alive and playing for those who died that damned night. I'd had better luck, music had saved my life and I hoped that *now,* my music would reach those thirty-two people, wherever they were.

I sobbed as the final round of applause erupted.

The Raphael Project

I dedicated two of my albums to the Victoria and Albert Museum: one is called **The Raphael Project** and the other simply **Museum**.

The Raphael Project is a piano suite in seven movements inspired by Raphael's *Cartoons*, a series of seven large-scale tempera drawings, considered one of the greatest treasures of the Renaissance.

Raphael's cartoons were originally models that were used to make tapestries to embellish the walls of the Sistine Chapel in the Vatican, but the pictorial quality prevailed over their original function, elevating them to absolute masterpieces of Renaissance art.

They were commissioned by Pope Leo X, shortly after his election in 1513 and depict the lives of the apostles Saint Peter and Saint Paul.

The genesis of my Raphael Project is quite singular and starts from Botticelli.

In March 2016 an incredible exhibition at the V&A entitled *Botticelli Reimagined* began, a tribute to the great influence that the brilliant Italian painter had on modern and contemporary culture. His iconic pictures are deeply ingrained in the collective unconscious, and his impact can be seen in everything from fashion to design, from cinema to entertainment in general.

The Botticelli Reimagined exhibition at the V&A offered a reinvention of his pictorial language by numerous artists and designers of our time, including David La Chapelle, Andy Warhol, Dante Gabriel Rossetti, Rene Magritte, Jeff Koons and others.

In short, quite a pop interpretation of the iconographic legacy of the great Italian artist.

Throughout the exhibition period, the V&A welcomed visitors at the entrance with a large installation in the shape of a large shell, a reproduction of the famous *Birth of Venus* by Botticelli, with the beautiful protagonist rising from the waters.

You could jump in the centre of the scallop shell, have your picture taken and pretend to be the goddess of love for a moment, a little mermaid and have your few seconds of glory on social media.

Word spread quickly and the Scallop soon became a performance on its own.

Before too long, the entire world was posing for a photo on that carousel.

Botticelli Reimagined was a huge success and the museum was packed with visitors every day.

As usual, I was playing the piano in the Gamble Room on a regular basis. During my breaks I would usually sit somewhere around the room but throughout the Botticelli exhibition, given the success and the enormous number of visitors, it was sometimes quite challenging to find a seat and so I would go to find a somewhat calmer place, away from the madding crowd.

My favourite secret retreat was the Raphael Room, one of the largest rooms in the museum and my cathedral of silence.

I sat and observed, enthralled.

Renaissance art has never been my favourite; I'm more inclined to contemporary languages of artistic expression, but those paintings by Raphael were really captivating me.

The size of the Cartoons, those evocative deeds and all the surrounding silence made my head implode somewhat.

I think I have been suffering from Stendhal Syndrome for a while. Those paintings had me completely spellbound.

Each scene felt like a musical tale.

And so I mentally began to step into those paintings, virtually experiencing the environmental sounds and voices of those characters up close: the prayer of the lame man healed in the temple, the screams for Ananias' death, the waves lapping and rocking the boats during the miraculous draught of fishes, the song of the birds flying over Lake Tiberias and the ones ashore, the chaos of the masses gathered for the sacrifice at Lystra…

Soon after, I began writing the musical themes inspired by those scenes in each of the seven Cartoons.

The **Raphael Project** began to take shape.

The result was a suite in seven movements, each movement dedicated to a cartoon.

I had made a connection with Raphael! My music allowed me a very personal interpretation and intimate access to his work.

In a few months I completed the project and the result thrilled me.

Between 2016 and 2017 I did a small tour with the **Raphael Project**. The first public performance was in the church of St. Giles in the Fields in London, the very same church I had previously hired for my **Inner Landscape** concert.

For the occasion, I had a screen set up close to the piano on which the images of Raphael's cartoons were projected during the concert.

Quite a memorable performance for me.

The **Raphael Project** album was recorded in Naples and released in April 2017.

I was very proud of myself!

I wanted to pay tribute to the Italian genius of Raphael and a tribute to the V&A, this magnificent museum that has his masterworks on permanent display.

Music let me transform, transfigure and miraculously inhabit unexplored worlds, such as that of Renaissance painting.

Museum

One of my favourite things to do on my long trips was making field recordings of the places I visited. It was like keeping a travel journal.

Environmental sound is really important to me. For example, I don't listen to music through headphones while travelling or walking. I want to immerse myself in the soundscape, capture the voices of the people and nature around me.

When I was working aboard the Costa Concordia cruise ship, I stored about 2000 gigabytes of field recordings into my hard disks. Captured with a portable recorder, those audio files were the most treasured memory of places I had visited around the world whilst cruising. One of my upcoming projects would have been to select and mix those sounds with my own piano music.
Unfortunately, during the shipwreck of the Concordia, I lost everything I had in my cabin. All that precious material ended up at the bottom of the sea.

All I had left with me was a pen, the ship Crew Member ID card and my life.
All those sounds and voices silenced forever. *Such a shame.*

But I never gave up on that idea of continuing with my field recordings and now I had a great opportunity. My work as a pianist in the historic café of such a great and popular museum gave me the privilege of immersing myself in an incredibly interesting cocktail of sounds.
Every day there were visitors from all over the world and being there to hear their voices and sounds was like travelling without moving from my piano.
Once upon a time I was off to see the world, I sailed the seven seas and played my piano around. Now, in that museum, I was sitting at my Kawai *and instead had the world coming to see me.*

I wanted to record the sound of the Victoria and Albert Museum, its sonic texture and mix it with my music.

The idea behind **Museum** was to disclose part of these precious sound memories to recreate my own collection of soundscapes.
It was like opening the doors to my own museum.

This adventure was full of surprises.
The predominant sound in the V&A is mainly produced by visitors, which changes according to the time of day. Voices and footsteps echo in the spacious rooms, the rhythmic comments of the tour guides, that long swarm of murmuring sounds hovering above groups of visiting tourists, the creak of a heavy door and its slamming.
The museum has its own sonic palette.

In the morning the sounds and voices resemble the slow awakening of a forest with rustling foliage gently blowing in the wind. The first visitors sound like curious birds exploring new territory. During the day the sound becomes more full-bodied in proportion to the gradual and increasing turnout.

The historic café of the Gamble Room is the final destination where all visitors converge after their excursions around the museum's many rooms.
I've always played there in the afternoon and, sitting at the piano, I was stunned by the variety of sounds of voices in different languages that accumulated like layers of coloured clouds all around.
At other times they resembled rushing torrents, or the ebb and flow of a tide.

When I was listening and with my recorder ready to use, I tried to trace the country of origin, the part of the world where a particular voice came from. It was really fascinating to rebuild an entire world starting from a sound.

During my breaks I often happened to exchange a few words with some random visitors.
One rainy November afternoon, a girl sat down at a table right next to the piano. She remained for a long time with her eyes closed and when she reopened them every now and then she hinted at a smile. I think she must have liked my music.
I took the opportunity to approach her and ask her to leave me a vocal note as a memory of her visit and experience. She told me she was Arab, accepted my invitation and recorded something without specifying the content.

She introduced herself as Ghadeer and left me a message in Arabic which I later translated with the help of a dear friend from Kuwait.
This is a fragment of the message I included in *Ghadeer (in love with a stranger)* the first track of my album **Museum**:
...then a foreigner appears and leaves an indelible mark inside you.

Mohammed, a guy from Bangladesh, was working as a waiter in the historic cafe where I played. Every now and then he would come up and ask me: "Do you know this Bangladeshi song?". I reluctantly answered no, but one day I made him a suggestion:
"Mohammed, why don't you sing me one?"
So, during a short break he came over to the piano, closed his eyes and sang me an ancient traditional melody from his country which I have recorded and included in **Museum**.

One day I met Francesca, a young Italian philosopher and talented artist. I was introduced to her through a mutual friend. She came to see me at the V&A and wrote something very poetic in one of her notebooks.
She told me that my music had created a powerful image in her head that day and she wanted to leave a voice message in Italian on my recorder. A sort of rather focused haiku that I included in my album. The image Francesca was talking about was this: *Nella sala un tramonto (A sunset in the room).*
She imagined the room where I played as a natural scenario where a large sun set placidly to the sound of my music.

Museum has been an incredible source of emotions.
Voices and sounds bring me news of other worlds and make me feel nostalgic for those places I've never seen or may never see. But for a moment I'm there and can live the

daydream of a wonderful journey that fills my heart with pure joy.

Museum is a caravan oasis where people meet for a short time, telling stories and bringing messages from distant places.

It was recorded in London in 2019.

Virus

I have adopted this sky for months.
Looking out the window and seeing those clouds moving, like drifting
sculptures, filled my heart with joy.
That sky was mine for a while.

March 2020.
I had just returned from a trip to Morocco.
The V&A was exhibiting *Wonderful Things,* a mesmerising journey into the visionary worlds created by photographer Tim Walker. An amazing collection of, at times, grotesque visual fairytales.
I saw it and found it really fascinating. I felt like stepping into one of his dramatic dreamscapes. He is a true magician.
It was the 5th of March. I would have expected a larger number of visitors at the museum, to be honest. Strange, I thought. The V&A is usually packed with people and Tim Walker normally attracts large crowds.
Anyway, his photographs left a long lasting ***wow*** effect on the faces of the lucky few.

However, there was quite an unprecedented atmosphere in London at the time.

I don't watch television but there was strange news everywhere: in far away China a rare form of epidemic never heard of before was causing trouble. Airports closing down, entire cities isolated, hospitals collapsing.

In London, passengers on the tube read the news and folded the newspaper with a shrug.

Well, I said to myself, *shit happens*. Luckily China is far from here.

The strange thing was that this news was more and more in the foreground and showed no sign of disappearing from newspapers, internet and TV.

On the contrary.

I exited the Tim Walker exhibition and headed towards the Gamble Room, the room where I normally work. I still had half an hour before starting to play.

Let's have a coffee then.

"Can you come to the office as soon as you can? I have to talk to you."

The manager at the museum looked around nervously.

What did he want from me?

"The number of visitors is decreasing more and more..." he told me.

The museum was emptying out and the restaurant business not doing well.

"You know, there's this virus thing, something they say comes from China.

Over here we still don't quite know what to do with the business, but what do you say if we suspend your service for a while?"
He anxiously tapped his pen on the table.
"Shall we do another week? I promise we'll call you back as soon as this story is over".

On the 13th of April 2013, I started this magical adventure at the V&A.
On 13th of March, 2020 I lost my job because of a virus.

The museum quickly shut its doors. I closed my piano lid, locked it and sadly walked away.

Suddenly we all found ourselves with our backs against the wall, isolated, fearful and insecure in the face of a planetary evil that had caught humanity by surprise.
Cities shut down one after another, the streets emptied, the world frozen in time.
The epidemic had become a pandemic and in a short time the COVID-19 virus had taken over the entire planet and was killing mercilessly.
A sinister and thick mantle fell over the world casting a pall of terror over our lives.
We found ourselves alone, facing exponentially growing death tolls on daily basis, learning about social distancing and a strange vocabulary of terms never heard before, which became unfortunately familiar. Like *LOCKDOWN*.
The ambulance sirens ripped the thick weave of that ominous mantle far and wide and for quite some time this was the sound that scratched our days like the edge of a sharp knife.

Humanity had descended into an abyss, into the dark depths of its night.

We found ourselves in a prison, with the monstrous image of that deadly virus always before our eyes.
An ancestral fear and a sinister symbolism: the virus attacked our breath, the divine breeze of life.

My life, like so many others, had fallen silent.

At Home

In March 2020 I had lost my job because of COVID 19 and I became more than a bit anxious. I didn't have many resources, no idea about what to do, nobody could move from home, only a stroll in the park was permitted and no social contacts.
It was the onset of a dreadful lockdown.
I called my parents in Italy to find out how they were. The situation was serious everywhere in the world.
It was a global paralysis.

Silence squatted on the days like a stultifying, ominously heavy cloud.

It was a new kind of silence, something none of us had ever experienced before.
But it was precisely in that silence that I gradually began to find something, something that kicked me off, awakening my dull senses, stunned by this unusual numbness.
The days were long, time was a still and vast lake whose shores I could not see.

Memories, sounds, voices, colours, dreams seemed buried under that silent mantle.

I began to dig into it to bring what I found back to the surface.

Every moment of the day was good for reflecting, listening, exploring. I composed music sitting on the bed, on the floor, at night, at the window, in the kitchen.

Music was emerging from the depths and literally taking me by storm.

Between March and April 2020 **At Home** was born, my first album entirely home recorded during the lockdown.

I found myself drawing on a surprising emotional archeology and the long period of the pandemic proved to be a great source of inspiration.

I am particularly fond of this project. Some of the tracks are very descriptive of my state of mind, such as *I'm dancing alone* in which I imagined dancing on top of the planet with everyone in a ritual dance of purification and healing from the virus.

Omnia mutantur (*everything changes* in Latin) is a reflection on the sudden change we all experienced in that period. A change that often takes place in the world without us realising it, but this time it was very rapid and took everyone by surprise.

My sailing piano has been inspired by my imaginary small piano-shaped boat with which I travel around the world, propelled by the light winds of music. My sailing piano has taken me around the world and together we have overcome and survived storms, shipwrecks, crises, loneliness and so on.

I know that it will save my life and take me to a safe harbour again.

At Home contains an important message for me: after an unprecedented event like the pandemic, I'm dreaming of a new Renaissance for humanity and the new awareness that we will have a better life.
After this horrible crisis we will regain the strength and the vitality that will make us look like birds in ecstatic murmuration.

Crescendo

*I'm here to paint music
in the dark*

During the pandemic I manifested another dream of mine: publishing a book of poetry.
I used to compose poetry for years without bothering to mention it to anyone. Most of the time they were drifting thoughts or sudden and abstract images that I reported in my many travel notebooks.

One of the obvious consequences of the COVID-19 pandemic has been isolation.
The virus had imprisoned us all and everyone reacted in some way to this forced condition.
In my case, I had lost my job, I didn't have a penny in my pocket, but I had a lot of time for myself.
London had become a ghost town, like so many others in the world.

After recording my album **At Home** I wanted to do something different, so I thought I'd tap into another source and blend it with the music.

I wanted to write poetry inspired by music. In fact I have always believed that there is poetry in music and music in poetry.

I didn't have in mind what to write about but slowly, in the silent corners of the day, **Crescendo** took shape.

Crescendo in music, as we know, is a gradual and progressive increase in sound volume. In my case I wanted to refer to more metaphorical directions of meaning: my inner world of sounds, images, colours, memories was materialising in a *crescendo* of emotional tension.
Musical terms have been precious travel tools that I have used to modulate and shape feelings giving them a direction, a sense of rhythm, an atmosphere.

I dreamed of imaginary vast spaces where anyone could sit and listen to the notes of my intimate and secret world.

The Word is Sound and through this Sound I explore my World.

I personally edited the Italian translation of this first collection of poems, composed between August and November 2020, originally written in English.
I loved giving space to the sound of the word, to the breath, to its evolution during the transition between the two languages, with the aim of re-creating identical atmospheres, despite the obvious differences.
Translating was not an easy task, but once again music came to the rescue and made a great contribution to the word, reinforcing an ancient bond.

My Antimosphere
Nine piano stories
Seven memories

here at the piano
bent over the keys
the soul is blowing on my fingers

For nine days, from February 15th to the 23rd 2021, I sat at the piano just before dinner and started improvising without knowing exactly what I was doing.
I love to improvise, I think it's pure magic. Create something without a structure, simply following the instinct. It is an unknown territory where I venture without knowing exactly where to go, a bit like slipping into tunnels without knowing where they lead.

I have defined this territory **Antimosphere**. It's my area, my inner world: fantastic, mysterious, unknown, surprising, where I venture like an explorer in a virgin forest.

In this album I wanted to tell nine stories on the piano, every night for nine days.

I have always liked telling stories and doing it with the help of my trusted friend, the piano, was quite exciting. We were like two old friends sitting by a fireplace in winter.

In my **Nine piano stories** you will hear what I found in my **Antimosphere**.
There is no plot, if not the random one created by the suggestion and the magic of the music.

Seven memories is another album in the **Antimosphere** series and is a work of deep intimacy. It was fully recorded during a short holiday in September 2022 at my parents' house in Recale, my small hometown in the south of Italy.
The occasion of the trip was my mother's birthday.
In the house where my parents live there's still my bedroom with all my memories, photos, letters, my old notebooks, music scores, books I loved to read.
One afternoon I sat down at my old piano in the room where I had lived for many years and recorded the **Antimosphere/ Seven memories** album in one take.

They are musical reflections and meditations on the things that are close to my
heart - my life, memories, dreams, thoughts and hopes - that were all born in that tiny room.
Music is a gateway to these memories and allows me to endlessly reconstruct my life, as well as relive that time and discover more about myself.

Both in **Nine piano stories** and in **Seven memories** I didn't want to add titles to the tracks.
Let your imagination run wild and free and give my *pianostories* a title if you wish.

Leave me a message

Time is now.
Your thoughts start swirling like whirlpools in the water.
Breathe.

The journey with my piano continues.
I still have stories to tell.

After the scary COVID-19 pandemic that broke out in 2020
the world is no longer what we knew, but a certain relative
serenity and hope seems to have been injected into our days
again.
This matter of the virus has made us acquire a new awareness
or at least reminded us of how powerful but also fragile life is.
Everyone experienced that period in their own way, but
something brought us together.
Death spread panic across the world during the pandemic and
there seemed to be no escape for us.

Many things have changed, many certainties dismantled. That monstrous virus seems to be under control now and we are back on the street to hug each other again (with caution) with faces a little tired but happy to still be here celebrating.

The world is constantly changing, we have to adapt like the water does on the river bed and keep the stream flowing downhill.

This is how I see life.

I still live in London and have resumed playing my piano at the V&A after a forced break of about fourteen months. Many return to greet me there, where I've been for more than ten years of my life and I certainly wouldn't wish to stop now.

...*How are you?* Great to see you again and hear you again!

I saw the lovely Amanda again, the Greek lady. She stopped near the far edge of the grand piano and blew me a kiss from a distance instead of her usual one on my forehead. "Do you remember Peter?"

"Sure, I remember". I already imagined that the news she was about to tell me would not be good.

She shrugged and rolled her eyes.

"Well...from now I'll be coming alone to listen to you. Rest in peace, Peter".

Every time I sit down at the piano and start playing in that museum, I always imagine that sooner or later someone will arrive, that they will come to me and tell me something and this will blow the sail of my piano away, like a magical wind of dreams.

I am grateful to life that has granted me this privilege of being here and share the miracle of music with the world.

When I started playing at the V&A again after the pandemic, I picked up a new habit. Everyone who comes to see me, will find a guest book on the piano lid, an album with blank pages that anyone who wants can fill with a memory of any kind.

Leave me a message I wrote on the first page.

I always want to treasure the memory of something, of someone. I've lived in different places, I've travelled a lot, who knows where I'll be tomorrow...

Everything is volatile and transitory. But I want something meaningful to stay and remain with me.

Leave me your message, your footprint, the sound of your passage, your voice.

Let the music of your life mix with mine. It's the memory, the memory is what we will always carry with us, the most precious treasure that no one will ever be able to steal. *Music for me is the guardian of this treasure.*

My pockets are empty, but my heart is full of joy because I live on music, which helps me to rebuild my memory every day, of what I have been and am.

I've been through very difficult times and ended up in the hospital on several occasions during the pandemic. I've had anxiety attacks, high blood pressure, breathing problems, insomnia. My private life has been heavily under the weather as well and there have been moments when the only thing I wanted to do was run away from everyone and everything, similarly to what happened to me after the accident with the ship.

Furthermore, this period had brought back some sediments of the trauma I had suffered after the shipwreck, even if there was no apparent connection between COVID and PTSD.

Free fall

I'm a tightrope walker up in the air.

One step at a time, that's how you walk every inch on the rope.
One step at a time.
My heart is pounding, the roll of the drum that sets my pace.
The foot touches the string, the foot feels it, the foot informs me.
The foot also knows that I have fallen and may fall again, *over and over again.*
But I won't be afraid this time. I am a man on a wire walking my time.

Ready.

I tumble among the stars
in the thin perfume of the night

mother hold me in your arms

father lift me in the air
the gravel crunches under my feet
my grandfather's tales
my first piano
the enchanted garden
my cousins knocking on the window
Bach, Mozart, Clementi
earthquake
Duran Duran, U2, Spandau Ballet
eyes without a face
my piano teachers
in the far away country
sunset in the room

Sitting at the piano
first note, right hand
left hand follows
notes roll, stop, expand, sit by my side
no words needed to tell
thousands of stories

Bent over the keys
My soul blows on my fingers
And blows me up there
back on the rope
The foot
the foot on the rope, the foot feels, the foot informs me

down again
free fall among the stars
towards the net
It's my world, my home, my breath, my image

New York
to gaze at the stars
the ship is sinking
I live in Peckham, London
can I play that piano?
my own private sky
virus and silence
inside me

fall into the net

That net is the music
it saved my life
and saves me every day.

My name is Antimo
I am sitting at the piano
bent over the keys
the soul is blowing on my fingers

Afterword

Piano Music menu

I've played so many piano pieces in my life. This a just personal selection, a sort of listening guide, of the ones I'm more fond of. From my early years to today.

Early years

J. S. Bach: *Minuet in G major BWV Anh 114*
W. A. Mozart: *Piano Sonata No 16 C major K 545*
M. Clementi: *Sonatina in C major, op. 36 no. 1*
F. Schubert: *Impromptu in E flat major op.90 n.2*
C. Debussy: *Children's Corner*

Growing up/ The Conservatory years

J. S. Bach: *Well-Tempered Clavier (books 1 & 2)*
W. A. Mozart: *Sonata in A minor k.310*
G.F. Handel: *Passacaglia*
L. Van Beethoven: *Waldstein Sonata*
F. Chopin: *Ballade 1st op.23 in G minor.*
R. Schumann: *Carnaval Op. 9*
J. Brahms: *Rhapsody op.79 n.2*
F. Liszt: *Years of pilgrimage:Vallée d'Obermann*
F. Liszt: *Mephisto Waltz*
J. Brahms: *Intermezzo op. 117 n.2*
C. Debussy: *Arabesques*
R. Strauss: *Sonata in B minor op.5*
E. Grieg: *Sonata in E minor op.7*
E. Satie: *Gymnopédies*
S. Rachmaninov: *Etudes Tableaux op.39*

S. Prokofiev: *Sonata n.7*
M. A. Balakirev: *Islamey*

B. Evans: *Time remembered*
P. Glass: *Metamorphosis*
R. Sakamoto: *Merry Christmas Mr. Lawrence*
M. Nyman: *The heart asks pleasure first*
L. Einaudi: *Le Onde*

My albums

Antimo Magnotta:
Inner Landscape
The Raphael Project
Museum
At Home
Antimosphere/ nine piano stories
Antimosphere/ seven memories

Acknowledgement

Heartfelt thanks to all those who believe in me, appreciate my music and my writings. I'm very grateful to Haldi Sheahan for her precious support and unvaluable help with the editing and to Rossella, a delicate creature with an immense heart.

Grazie

Antimo

Antimo Magnotta is an Italian musician and author based in London

www.antimomagnotta.com

Books By This Author

The Pianist of Costa Concordia

The account of the Costa Concordia shipwreck, which ran aground on the 13th of January 2012 claiming 32 lives, as reported by the Italian pianist Antimo Magnotta who was aboard that fateful night and miraculously survived.

This is an intimate chronicle of life on board the infamous cruise ship, leading up to its catastrophic demise, as seen through the perceptive eyes of one of the key performers on board.

The cruise vessel is depicted as a theatre of glamour and delusion which can both lead to new relationships or closure on others, as the passengers confide their personal narratives to those willing to listen.

The pianist plays a major role here and readers are able to share the advancing horror of the situation and taste the bitter aftermath.

Crescendo

There's poetry in music and music in poetry.

This adage is the best presentation for "crescendo", Antimo Magnotta's first work of poetry

He's a musician who turns to writing as a means of sorting through his inner landscape of sounds, images, colours, memories where life secretly and musically unfolds before his heart in a crescendo of ever ascending emotional tension.

Antimo Magnotta's poetry offers open wide spaces where you can have a sit and listen to him playing with words, tickling the ivories of his intimate, secret world.

HOW MUSIC SAVED MY LIFE

By Antimo Magnotta

Printed in Great Britain
by Amazon

22257534R00076